PLEASE WASH YOUR HANDS
BEFORE YOU READ ME!

DATE DUE			
JAN 31 '95	FEB 2 '99		
MAR 29 '95	APR 12 '99		
MAY 26 '95	NOV 11		
29 9	FEB 24 99		
SEP 19 95	NOV 26		
MAR 27 '96			
APR 26 '96			
NOV 29 '96			
FEB 26 97			
MAR 19 97			
APR 09 98			
APR 07 98			

23

A GOLDEN JUNIOR GUIDE®

CARDINALS, ROBINS,
and OTHER BIRDS

By GEORGE S. FICHTER

Illustrated by PATRICIA TOPPER

Consultant: Dr. Stephen W. Kress, Research Biologist, National Audubon Society, and Laboratory Associate, Laboratory of Ornithology at Cornell University

A GOLDEN BOOK • NEW YORK

Western Publishing Company, Inc., Racine, Wisconsin 53404

All Birds have two legs, two wings, a bill, and thousands of feathers. Feathers distinguish birds from all other animals. They make it possible for most birds to fly. They also keep birds warm in cold weather and dry when it rains. And most people think feathers make birds beautiful. In this book you'll meet a variety of commonly seen or familiar birds and learn some fascinating facts about their behavior.

Most Birds shed all of their feathers once a year. This is called *molting*. But only a few flight feathers are shed at a time. This way, the bird can continue flying.

American Robin

crown

eye

bill

throat

back

breast

rump

wing

belly

tail

leg

toes

Did You Know?
There are about 100 billion birds on Earth. That's 25 times more birds than people!

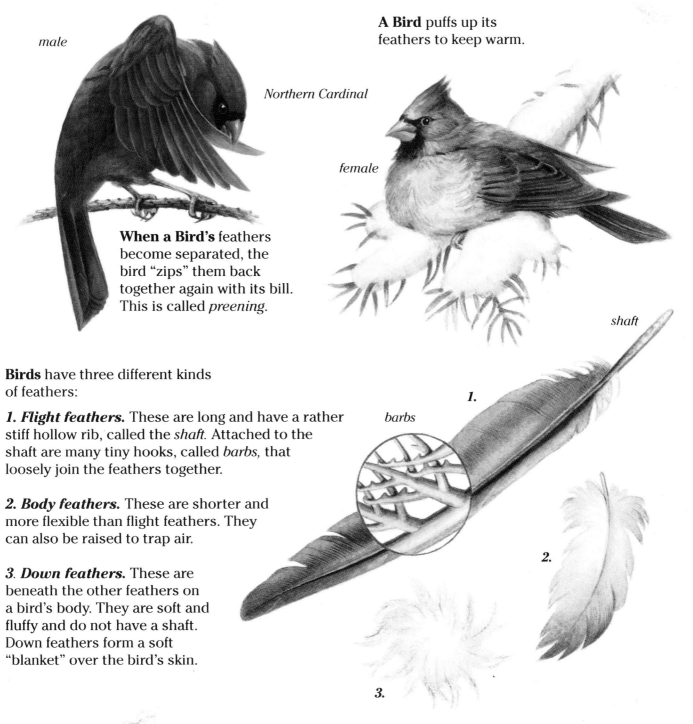

male

Northern Cardinal

A Bird puffs up its feathers to keep warm.

female

When a Bird's feathers become separated, the bird "zips" them back together again with its bill. This is called *preening*.

shaft

barbs

1.

2.

3.

Birds have three different kinds of feathers:

1. Flight feathers. These are long and have a rather stiff hollow rib, called the *shaft.* Attached to the shaft are many tiny hooks, called *barbs,* that loosely join the feathers together.

2. Body feathers. These are shorter and more flexible than flight feathers. They can also be raised to trap air.

3. Down feathers. These are beneath the other feathers on a bird's body. They are soft and fluffy and do not have a shaft. Down feathers form a soft "blanket" over the bird's skin.

Birds are different from each other not only in size, shape, and color but also in what they eat. For some clues to what a bird eats and how it obtains its food, look at its feet and bill. For example, all birds have four toes. But birds that catch their food on the ground or on the wing and bring it back to a perch have three toes facing forward and one facing backward.

American Robin

Robins are birds that perch. Right after they land on the branch, they curl their toes around it. This locks them into place and keeps the bird from falling.

Woodpecker bill

A Cardinal uses its thick cone-shaped bill to crack the hard covers on seeds. It then eats the soft kernels inside.

Hummingbird bill

Robin bill

Northern Cardinal

Cardinal bill

4

A Woodpecker has a straight, sharp bill. It uses it to dig into the bark of trees to find hidden insects.

Ruby-throated Hummingbird

A Hummingbird has a long, narrow bill. With it the hummingbird can sip the sweet fluid, called *nectar*, from flowers.

Downy Woodpecker

Did You Know?

Birds do not have teeth. After they swallow their food, it is ground up by muscles in a special part of their stomach called the *gizzard*. Birds also sometimes store food in a throat pouch called the *crop*. This food may be eaten later or brought to the nest and fed to the young.

Woodpeckers have two toes facing forward and two toes facing backward. This helps them to climb and hold on to trees.

5

Cardinal males are bright red all over, including the feathery crest on top of their head. Their bill is pinkish red, with a black "mask" covering part of it. Females and young birds are brownish in color, with a little red. Both males and females have a loud, cheery song they sing in early spring and summer. They use it to attract a mate and to announce their arrival back home. Cardinals are usually calm and peaceful. But they will fight fiercely to defend their territory.

sleeping

Cardinals sleep like most other birds, by turning their head around and tucking their bill into their shoulder feathers.

Northern Cardinal

male

Cardinals often visit bird feeders in winter. Their favorite food is sunflower seeds. But they feed insects to their young.

female

young

Did You Know?
The Cardinal, like most other birds, cools off by opening its mouth and panting.

Female Cardinals lay three or four eggs at a time, all beige or pale green with brownish spots. Each female may raise two families a year.

7

American Goldfinches,

with their notched, or V-shaped, tail, are also known by the nickname of Wild Canaries. This is due to the male's bright yellow color in summer. Goldfinches usually travel in flocks. They will often come to bird feeders offering sunflower or thistle seeds. The Goldfinch's steep, wavelike motions make the bird easy to recognize as it flies high up in the sky.

The American Goldfinch male has a black forehead and black wings. In winter the male's yellow color becomes dull, almost gray. Females and young are duller in color all year long.

American Goldfinch

female

male

Female Goldfinches, like most female birds, will lay a new group of eggs if the first is destroyed by wind or predators.

White-breasted Nuthatches usually come down trees headfirst. They search the bark for spiders and insects. They also wedge seeds into cracks in the bark, then peck at the seeds to remove their outer covering. Sometimes nuthatches come to bird feeders in search of one of their favorite foods—hardened fat called *suet*. Male and female White-breasted Nuthatches look similar, although the crown on males is black. On females it is gray. The call of the Nuthatch sounds like: "Yank, yank, yank!"

male White-breasted Nuthatch

The White-breasted Nuthatch has a long, sharp bill. As it searches for insects, it balances itself by holding its short tail stiff and straight. It rarely comes to the ground.

black crown

Did You Know?

A bird held in your hand feels very warm. This is because its body temperature is over 105 degrees Fahrenheit (F). A person's is normally 98.2 degrees F. To keep up its temperature, a bird must eat most of the time it is awake.

9

House Sparrows can be seen nearly everywhere that people live. These familiar birds are found all over—in cities, on farms, in suburbs and parks, probably even in your own backyard. Males have a black throat and chest and white cheeks. The top of their head is gray. Females and young birds are streaked with brown and gray.

Bluebirds

female

House Sparrow

House Sparrows like to build nests in protected places. They sometimes take over birdhouses built for other birds. Their nests are made of grass, weeds, leaves, feathers, and often trash.

A House Sparrow's favorite foods are insects and seeds. In cities the birds sometimes feed on garbage.

male

Sparrows, like most birds, take baths regularly. They may bathe in water, dust, or both. Bathing helps them get rid of lice and other insect pests.

11

Blue Jays are big, bold, and noisy. They scream and call loudly: "Jay, jay, jay!" But they also have a soft, pretty song that they usually sing when hidden in the bushes. Males and females look alike. Their wings, back, and crest are bright or grayish blue. The young look very similar to their parents.

Did You Know?
Blue Jays will often chase bigger birds, such as hawks or owls, away from feeders. They will sometimes even chase away dogs or cats.

Blue Jay

The Blue Jay has a handsome pointed crest, which usually stands up.

Blue Jays will eat spiders, insects, fruits, and acorns. Like squirrels, they tuck extra acorns into hiding places. Some of the acorns sprout and grow into trees!

American Crow

Blue Jay

The Blue Jay is a close relative of the much larger American Crow, which is black. A Blue Jay's wings are shorter, though. The American Crow's wings reach nearly to the tip of its tail.

European Starlings

are plump, short-tailed birds that often travel together in huge flocks. These glossy black birds were first brought to the United States from Europe about 100 years ago. Now they live all over the country!

The Starling's bill is bright yellow in spring and summer. In winter it turns dark.

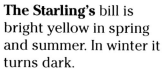

summer

winter

European Starling

Starlings will eat almost anything, from ants and beetles to berries and fruits. In cities, they will eat whatever they can find, picking through litter and raiding garbage cans.

Starlings rest together, or *roost*, in large flocks in trees or on rooftops. These noisy gatherings may contain thousands of birds.

Did You Know?
Starlings can fly up to 55 miles an hour. That's twice as fast as most other commonly seen birds.

Titmice and Chickadees

Titmice and Chickadees usually flock together in winter and are regular visitors to bird feeders. The Tufted Titmouse is easily recognized by its pointed crest. With its gray back, white chest, and orange patches, the young Tufted Titmouse is quite similar in appearance to the adult. The Black-capped Chickadee has a black cap and a black "bib" on its throat. It is smaller than the Tufted Titmouse.

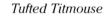

Tufted Titmouse

The Tufted Titmouse gives a clear two-note whistle, then quickly repeats it: "Pe-ter, Pe-ter, Pe-ter."

The Chickadee calls its name again and again: "Chickadee-dee-dee, chickadee-dee-dee."

Black-capped Chickadee

Did You Know?
Chickadees are so friendly, they will sometimes eat right out of your hand. Tufted Titmice are not as tame.

Chickadees often hang upside down on branches or feeders to eat.

17

Northern Oriole

Northern Oriole males are among the most colorful of all the birds you will see in your backyard. They have patches of bright orange on their body and tail. The head, throat, and shoulders are jet black. Females are less striking. They are olive or brown where the males are black. Also, the orange on their chest and belly is paler.

female

Oriole nests, which look like burlap sacks, hang near the ends of tree branches. You can give the birds pieces of string or yarn to weave into their nests.

Northern Oriole

Orioles often move about in the treetops calling to each other. Their call sounds like a flute.

18

Did You Know?
Like many other birds, Orioles fly south to warmer places in winter, then return north in the spring to make their nests. This is called *migration*. Some North American birds, such as the Chimney Swift, fly all the way to South America and back every year!

male

19

Carolina Wrens like to be near people. Their loud, clear call, repeated throughout the day, sounds like: "Tea-kettle, tea-kettle, tea-kettle!" Carolina Wrens eat mainly insects. Since they do not fly south for the winter, those birds living in the north may die if the winter is especially long and cold, and food becomes scarce.

Carolina Wren

A Carolina Wren can be identified by the large white line above its eye and by its rust-colored back.

Did You Know?

Carolina Wrens sometimes build their nests in funny places. For example, you might find one in an open mailbox or in the pocket of a pair of pants hanging from a clothesline!

Wrens may carry their short, rounded tail straight up. Or, they may tilt it in toward their head.

nest with young

Did You Also Know?

Dull colors help a nesting bird hide from predators. Both male and female Wrens are dull in color, so they can take turns sitting on the eggs. A brightly colored male bird, like the Cardinal, does not help the female keep the eggs warm.

21

American Robins are familiar orange-breasted birds. They make themselves at home on lawns and in gardens. There you may see them running along the ground for short distances. Often they will pause and cock their head to one side, looking for food. Then they will make a quick stab with their bill to pick up a worm or an insect. You may also see them picking at berries or fruits.

Male Robins have a black head and neck. Females and young birds are grayer. The young birds have black spots on their breast, like other members of the Thrush family.

American Robin

male

young

Did You Know?
Young robins grow very fast. Just 14 days after hatching, they are nearly as large as their parents!

female

egg tooth

Baby Robins, like other baby birds, cut their way out of their shell using a structure called an *egg tooth*. This tiny tooth on the tip of their bill soon falls off. The baby birds do not have feathers. To stay warm, they must be fed often. Both parents help to feed them.

Robins make nests out of twigs and grass held together with mud. If there is no mud nearby, they will make mud by filling their bill with dust and dipping it in water. It takes them about a week to make the nest.

23

Mockingbirds and Catbirds

are close relatives. Both can imitate other birds. But a mockingbird is by far the better "mocker." Mockingbirds can imitate the sounds of a squeaky gate, a barking dog, a whistle, and a crowing rooster! They are slightly larger than Catbirds and have white on their wings and tail. Catbirds are plain gray, with a black cap on their head and a dark orange patch under their tail.

Mockingbirds, in spring, sometimes sing all night long. They may change their tune several times in a minute.

Northern Mockingbird

Did You Know?

Mockingbirds and Catbirds usually eat insects. This helps farmers control insect pests. But the birds also eat fruits and berries. When these food items ripen, the birds themselves may become the pests!

The Catbird's call sounds like the cries of a mewing cat. In fact, that's where this bird's name comes from!

Gray Catbird

Did You Also Know?

All birds have at least 14 bones in their neck. Mammals—even long-necked giraffes —have only 7.

Downy Woodpeckers

are less than 6 inches long and have a white stripe down their back. They are the smallest woodpeckers in the United States and also the friendliest. They can often be seen at feeders alongside Chickadees. Sometimes Hairy Woodpeckers, which look similar to Downy Woodpeckers, will also appear, but they are more timid. Woodpeckers eat mainly insects they find crawling on trees.

*male
Downy Woodpecker*

The Hairy Woodpecker is a little bigger than the Downy Woodpecker. Also, its bill is as long as its head. The Downy's bill is only half as long as its head.

Hairy

Woodpeckers may peck holes in a tree to get to the beetles burrowing inside. Stiff tail feathers help the bird to prop itself up against the tree trunk.

Downy

26

Downy and Hairy Woodpecker males have a small red patch on the back of their head. Females do not have this patch.

male Hairy Woodpecker

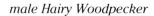

barbed tip of tongue

A Woodpecker's long tongue has tiny hooks, or barbs, on its tip for spearing insects.

27

Flickers are big, brownish woodpeckers. Their back is covered with black streaks. They have a black "bib" and also a bright red mark on the back of their neck. Males and young birds have a black "mustache."

Male Flickers flash their white rump when they fly. They also show the bright yellow feathers that are under their wings.

male

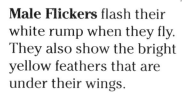

Common Flicker

"bib"

"mustache"

Flickers, unlike most other woodpeckers, do most of their hunting for ants and other tasty insects on the ground. However, you might occasionally find one looking for food on the trunk of a tree.

female feeding young

nest in tree hole

Female Woodpeckers lay their eggs in holes bored into trees. Their eggs are white. In contrast, eggs laid in open nests are usually colored or speckled. This helps them blend in with their surroundings.

Woodpecker egg

Red-winged Blackbird egg

Did You Know?
Male woodpeckers like to hammer noisily on dead branches or metal pipes to announce: "Here is where I live. Keep away!"

29

Ruby-throated Hummingbird

Ruby-throated Hummingbird males have a brilliant red throat. The throats of females and young birds are white with pale brown spots. Hummingbirds can hover motionlessly in front of flowers while they feed. Then they fly off at incredibly fast speeds. Their wings beat so rapidly, they make a humming noise. But all you can see is a blur!

male

Ruby-throated Hummingbird

Hummingbirds feed on nectar. They sip it from flowers with their long, slim bill. Their favorite flowers are tube-shaped and bright red.

Did You Know?
Hummingbirds can fly forward, backward, sideways, straight up, or straight down!

30

The Female lays two eggs in a tiny, cup-shaped nest neatly woven from soft leaves and grasses. The nest is held together with spider silk the bird gathers.

female

Did You Also Know?
Most birds have hollow bones. This helps reduce the bird's weight for flying.

The Hummingbird's egg (shown here actual size) is about the size of a pea. It is the smallest of all birds' eggs.

Chimney Swifts

Chimney Swifts chatter and twitter as they fly around trying to catch insects. Their narrow, slightly curved wings are very long. The birds are dark gray in color, like the inside walls of chimneys. Hundreds or even thousands of Chimney Swifts roost in chimneys at night and build their nests there. They fly all day and do not stop to rest until evening.

Chimney Swift

Chimney Swifts have a short bill and a mouth that opens wide. This allows them to catch insects in flight.

Did You Know?
Chimney Swifts like to travel in flocks. They are often seen with Swallows, which they resemble.

Chimney Swifts don't perch on tree branches. Instead, they cling to the sides of walls and chimneys using their short, stiff tail as a prop.

Chimney Swift nests are made of twigs and are held together with the bird's saliva, which acts like a glue. Saliva is also used to attach the nest to the side of the chimney.

Chimney Swifts drink while in flight. They lower their head and, with an open beak, skim the surface of a pond or pool.

33

Mourning Doves, like Chimney Swifts, travel together in flocks. They can often be seen in gardens and yards. Although related to pigeons, they have a much slimmer body and a longer, more pointed tail. Mourning Doves are very fast fliers. If you listen carefully, you can hear the whistling noise of their wings in flight. Their body feathers are brownish gray with a few small black spots. The edges of the tail are white.

Mourning Doves

Tree Sparrow

Black-capped Chickadee

The Mourning Dove's call is a low, soft, cooing sound. It seems quite "mournful," or sad.

Young Mourning Doves are fed partly digested food that the adult bird has previously eaten and then spit up.

female feeding its young

Did You Know?
Mourning Dove nests, made loosely of twigs, are fragile. The wind often blows them off the branches, and the eggs or young birds fall to the ground. The eggs are destroyed, and the baby birds usually die. But most Mourning Doves still seem able to raise two or three families every year.

For Further Reading

With this book, you've only just begun to explore some exciting new worlds. Why not continue to learn about the wonderful creatures known as birds? For example, you might want to browse through *Birds* and *Bird Life* (both *Golden Guides*), which contain many fascinating details on the birds in this book and additional ones as well. Another Golden Book you might enjoy is *I Wonder How Parrots Can Talk and Other Neat Facts About Birds.* Also, be sure to visit your local library, where you will discover a variety of titles on the subject.

Index

Barbs, 3, 27
Bathing, 11
Bill, 4, 5, 6, 9, 14, 23, 26, 30, 32
Birdhouse, 10
Bird feeder, 6, 8, 9, 16, 26
Birds, features of, 2-3, 4-5
Body feathers, 3
Body temperature, 9
Bones, 25, 31

Canary, Wild, 8
Cardinal, 4, 6-7, 21
Catbird, 24-25
Chickadee, Black-capped, 16-17
Chimney Swift, 19, 32-33
Clutch, 8
Crop, 5
Crow, American, 13

Dove, Mourning, 34-35
Down, 3
Drinking, 33

Eggs, 7, 8, 21, 29, 31
Egg tooth, 23

Feathers, 2-3
Feet, 4
Flicker, 28-29
Flight, 30, 34,
    feathers, 3
    speed, 15
Food, 4, 8, 9, 11, 13, 14, 25, 26, 28, 30

Gizzard, 5
Goldfinch, American, 8

Hummingbird, 4, 5
    Ruby-throated, 30-31

Jay, Blue, 12-13

Migration, 19
Mockingbird, 24-25
Molting, 2

Nectar, 5, 30
Nest, 10, 18, 21, 23, 31, 33, 35
Nuthatch, White-breasted, 9

Oriole, 18-19

Perch, 4
Pigeon, 34
    milk, 35
Preening, 3

Robin, American, 4
Roost, 15

Saliva, 33
Shaft, 3
Singing, 12, 24
Sleep, 6, 15
Sparrow, House, 10-11
Starling, European, 14-15
Suet, 9
Swift, Chimney, 19, 32-33

Temperature, body, 9
Titmouse, Tufted, 16
Toes, 4, 5
Tongue, 27

Woodpecker, 4-5, 28-29
    Downy, 26-27
    Hairy, 26-27
Wren, Carolina, 20-21